THE LADY IN WHITE

The Lady in White

(La dame blanche)

❦

CHRISTIAN BOBIN

Translated by Alison Anderson

University of Nebraska Press ❦ *Lincoln and London*

Cet ouvrage publié dans le cadre du programme d'aide à la publication bénéficie du soutien du Ministère des Affaires Etrangères et du Service Culturel de l'Ambassade de France représenté aux Etats-Unis.

This work received support from the French Ministry of Foreign Affairs and the Cultural Services of the French Embassy in the United States through their publishing assistance program.

Cet ouvrage a bénéficié du soutien des Programmes d'aide à la publication de l'Institut Français.

This work, published as part of a program of aid for publication, received support from the Institut Français.

Publication of this book was assisted by a grant from the National Endowment for the Arts.

ART WORKS.

National Endowment for the Arts
arts.gov

Library of Congress Cataloging-in-Publication Data
Bobin, Christian.
[Dame blanche. English]
The lady in white / Christian Bobin; translated by Alison Anderson.
pages cm
ISBN 978-0-8032-4565-5 (paperback: alk. paper)
ISBN 978-0-8032-6688-9 (epub)
ISBN 978-0-8032-6689-6 (mobi)
ISBN 978-0-8032-6690-2 (pdf) 1. Dickinson, Emily, 1830–1886—Fiction. I. Anderson, Alison, translator. II. Title.
PQ2662.O252D3613 2014   843'.914—dc23
2014013292

Set in Vendetta by Renni Johnson.
Designed by A. Shahan.

THE LADY IN WHITE

SHORTLY BEFORE SIX O'CLOCK IN THE MORNING, on May 15, 1886, as birdsong burst forth in the garden, rinsing the pink sky, and jasmine blessed the air with its perfume, the sound stopped at last. The sound that for two days had hampered all thought in the Dickinson home, a sound of gasping, labored, valiant breathing, like a saw rasping over a stubborn plank. Emily had suddenly turned her face to the invisible sun; for two years, it had been consuming her soul as if it were frail incense paper. Death filled the entire room, all at once.

This was an era when affluent families were in the habit of competing with the Eternal by taking photographs of their dead. There would be no photographs that day, only a few words of relief from those who were close, and their surprise upon seeing how white Emily's face was, similar to the light that pours forth from a lily.

Poetry is the sickly daughter of the heavens, the silent defeat of the world and its science. Dr. Bigelow did not write his prescription until he had seen his patient lying in her bed, dressed in white. He was not allowed to go into the room and would make his diagnosis while standing on the threshold. Emily was fifty-five years old. No one in the town of Amherst had seen her face for a quarter of a century.

THE WAR OF THE LIVING NEVER CEASED: Susan, Emily's much-loved sister-in-law, lived a hundred yards away, but she would not attend the funeral, because her husband, Austin, Emily's brother, had invited his mistress, Mabel Todd. Before the adulterous couple arrived, Susan dressed Emily in her final white armor, then withdrew. The whiteness of her freshly ironed mortuary gown splattered the darkness of the green-shuttered room. For years Emily had raised a fence of white linen between herself and the world. In the ground floor library was a copy of Tennyson's *Saint Agnes' Eve*, with her own annotations. It is the story of a nun, "in raiment white and clean," waiting for her "Sabbaths of Eternity." Deep in the sky a timepiece had stopped ticking. Hiding behind death, a woman who had never harmed another waited in her robes of snow for what would happen next.

She was laid carefully in a white coffin, then taken down to the hall of her father's home. The door was thrown open onto the sun-struck garden. Dozens of butterflies lightened the suffocating blueness of the sky. Golden drones—which Emily had wrenched from their destiny as slaves by crowning them in her poems—hummed a requiem.

Emily's sister, Vinnie, placed two fragrant white heliotropes in the dead woman's crossed hands, "to be given to Judge Lord," whom Emily loved. On the lid of the closed coffin were several fresh violets, and ferns in their crinkled serenity. The pastor of Amherst read a psalm, Reverend Jenkins expedited a prayer, and Colonel Higginson, the chilly discoverer of Emily's genius, recited Emily Brontë's last poem, which opens with a declaration of dauntlessness in the face of the darkness: "No coward soul is mine." As an adolescent Emily Dickinson recited this poem to her sister in the darkness of their bedroom, before going to sleep:

> There is not room for Death
> Nor atom that his might could render void
> Since thou art Being and Breath
> And what thou art may never be destroyed.

Nothing else would be said.

Six Irish servants, some of whom used to help Emily with her work in the rose garden—Dennis Scanlon, Orven Courtney, Pat Ward, Dennis Cashman, Dan Moynihan, and the one Emily called "the gracious stable boy," Stephen Sullivan—hoisted the coffin onto their sinewy shoulders and went through the rear door, where the shutters were opened wide and winglike against the brick wall, and after they had made their way through the barn with its gold-striped shadows, they strode into the tall grass buzzing with insects, doing everything as Emily had instructed for the day of her burial: they must go to the cemetery by way of the fields, without using the street.

"When it shall come my turn, I want a buttercup." Emily's wish had been fulfilled: the field behind the house was ablaze with thousands of buttercups. The field belonged to the Dickinsons; even in death she did not leave her home, and moved without transition from the writing room to the ditch the Amherst grave-digger had dug in the earth with his shining shovel.

A LITTLE GIRL WAS WATCHING AS the Irish giants crossed the blazing field with the white box on their shoulders. The little girl was six years old. She was the daughter of Mabel Todd, Emily's brother's mistress. Her mother was there, in the procession. The child—her name was Millicent—watched the mourners as they walked slowly and unsteadily beneath the cynical sun toward the cemetery, where a piece of earth had opened its jaws, ready to swallow the wooden coffin and the flesh of the dead woman.

Little Millicent could not bear her mother's love affair. In her sorrow she pictured the Dickinsons in the stormy colors of characters out of a tale: walking behind the coffin were "the witch," Vinnie, with her gnarled arms "like the bundles of firewood in the logpile," and "the king," Austin, whom Millicent had often seen in her own home, frowning as he sat by the fireplace with his mistress, kindling the flames with his cane—its knob was "a golden head."

At the age of six you have your nose glued to the window of what is real. You can see only a few details; your breath creates too much mist. Millicent did not have many images of Emily. The little girl recalled a mysterious redheaded lady in white who never left the house. From time to time a shutter would open slightly in the upstairs bedroom, and the lady would lower a wicker basket at the end of a rope. In the basket, piping hot from the oven, was gingerbread for a little neighbor.

The only favor the world ever showed Emily was in October 1856, to award her second prize at the Amherst fair for her rye bread.

The perfect word, each time it is found, illuminates the mind as if someone had pressed a switch inside one's skull. Writing is its own reward.

She was fifty-five years old. She hid her face as often as she could; she wanted to be seen by God alone since she could not be seen by her mother, then she died, and the first child who came along watched, unmoved, as her coffin made its way across a meadow electric with bees. There is always a stranger watching our death, and the carefree regard of that witness makes our passing a peaceful, Sunday-best sort of event, an event granted to the enigmatic procession of simple days.

In the cemetery, pines and ferns provided shade for the Dickinson family plot. Flowers were scattered over the coffin the moment it was lowered into the grave, and then everyone left. The heliotropes in the dead woman's hands shone in the dark.

A few hours went by, hours that were nothing. Time does not enter the home of the dead. A sun burst noiselessly inside the coffin, where suddenly it was brighter than noon.

FIFTY-THREE YEARS EARLIER: THE SKY ABOVE Amherst clouded over, as at Christ's death. A storm burst while a carriage was passing through a pine forest. Lightning peppered the trees, the devils behind the deluge bombarded the roof of the carriage, and it was forced to come to a halt. Inside was little Emily, two and a half years old; her mother, about to give birth to Vinnie, was sending Emily to spend a month with her aunt Lavinia. The child looked out at the apocalypse and begged her aunt: "Take me home to my mother, take me home to my mother." Dying soldiers call out like this, and no one answers them. Nor did anyone answer the little two-and-a-half-year-old warrior lost on the battlefield of the world. Then suddenly, huddled in the corner on the leather seat, she became supernaturally quiet. "If you do not swallow your death and your fear all at once, you will never come to anything good," says Saint Teresa of Avila. That was what the abandoned child had just done: her terror of the great rush of water, her mother's irreparable silence—she had just swallowed them all at once. The devils departed to shake their fists elsewhere; the sky shone admirably—the journey could continue.

There was a piano at Aunt Lavinia's house. The notes that emerged were like cherry blossoms—atoms of light cleansing the air, cleansing the heart. Emily was allowed to run her fingers over the keyboard. From time to time she spoke of her parents and "little Austin" but showed no wish to see them. Between absence and death there is no difference. She had lost all her loved ones and wore her mourning bravely, trying not to be a burden. She was not a problem, except one Sunday, when they took her to worship and she talked too loudly; she was rewarded with a slap.

The black baptism of abandonment left Emily as invulnerable as the dead. When you have lost everything, you can save everything. In her presence souls ignited like rosebushes; in the evening, when it was time for bed, she radiated such tranquility that her aunt liked to lie down alongside her for a few minutes—as if robbing a saint of her meager peace, touching a patch of her gown.

Aunt Lavinia, when sending news, wrote that the child "runs up to me at the slightest care." Later Emily would confide with angelic brutality that she never had a mother and that she "supposed" a mother was someone "to whom you hurry when you are troubled." It is the perfect definition of a mother. The best way to know something is through its absence.

EDWARD DICKINSON HAD A WOODEN HEAD, a forward-thrusting chin, two black eyes that searched and judged and condemned you but that, in the end, never looked at you. They were Old Testament eyes. The Bible is a fisherman's hut on the banks of the Eternal, with two rooms. In the first, the father is holding a slate on which he records all our omissions. In the second, the son is holding a sponge to wipe the slate clean. One Sunday morning, with the family standing to attention, ready to proceed royally along the path to church, the God of the Old Testament noticed that Emily was missing. Not until one hour later would she be found, in the cellar, reading a book whence a light clearer than that of an Easter morning arose—one of those books like *The Confessions of an Opium Eater* that Edward had bought for his daughter, warning her all the while not to read them, for fear they might trouble her. Emily's father was the type of man on whom the world rested, capable not only of providing for his family's comfort but also of governing a faraway province and ensuring that three crosses had been duly delivered to Golgotha for Friday afternoon, as requested by the imperial administration he served with such impeccable devotion. Treasurer of Amherst College, lawyer, senator: the medals dangling from his name jingled with every step he took. He could imagine no salvation elsewhere than in sleepless toil. "Let us prepare for a life of rational happiness [...] I anticipate pleasure from engaging with my whole soul in my business": thus did he woo his wife. In his soul he was a man of law. Nothing, to his way of thinking, could ever be made clear enough. When of an evening he opened his door to guests, he waved a lantern in front of their faces, although there was always a lamp burning in the entryway. When he converted to the new church, the minister took notice of this soul with its excess of polish: "You approach Christ as a man of law—you ought to go as a sinner, rather, on your knees." A Dickinson, on his knees? Edward preferred to plant his legs firmly on the ground, and with one hand acting as a visor, scan the skies in search of the copper plaque where God's name was engraved along with the list of his honorary titles.

THE FOOTBRIDGE OF LIFE CREAKED under young Emily's step: in 1852 death poached many souls around her, a quick blow to the neck before stuffing them still warm into its game bag. Some were Emily's close friends: Abby Haskell, nineteen years of age; Jennie Grout, twenty-one; Martha Kingman, twenty-one. Emily stepped quickly across the footbridge; it groaned uneasily. The following year, death would devour a regal dish: Benjamin Newton, her father's secretary. Benjamin was nine years older than Emily. He had spoken to her of the sweetness of invisible things; he lent her books and encouraged her to write. She called him "Master," thus awarding him the royal ermine of a title she always conferred upon men older than herself and in whose presence her sovereign soul flirted with abdication. But there are no masters before death. "I had a friend, who taught me Immortality—but venturing too near, himself—he never returned." When Benjamin collapsed, the flame he had been holding and that illuminated Emily's soul rolled into the void.

That same year, thanks to her father's tenacity, Amherst was at last linked by rail to the other towns in the region. The entire village gathered at the station to celebrate the arrival of the iron horse with its nostrils of soot. The father was all-powerful, the locomotive was all-powerful, everyone was celebrating this all-powerful demonstration in order to exorcise the imminence of death. They made speeches, tossed their hats into the air, shouted, exulted. They were drunk on progress. Emily watched her father's triumph from a distance. What became of the admirers of the locomotive, we do not know. They died even before their top hats, tossed to the sky, fell again into the dust; the hawk of the Eternal swooped down upon its prey, and their naïve submission doomed them to disaster. About the contemplative woman of Amherst we know more—we know that death would be at great pains to find her, and to flee from death, Emily hid behind God. To no avail, of course, for God is the secret name of death. Emily knew this, but it was simply a matter of taste: either one worshipped the world (money, glory, noise), or one worshipped life (a stray thought, a soul's untouched wilderness, a robin's courage). It was just a matter of taste.

WHEN ON THE THRESHOLD OF SLEEP Edward Dickinson closed his accounting books and opened the spacious register of his soul, all he saw was a blank page: no entries, no withdrawals.

"Father's real life and mine sometimes come into collision, but as yet, escape unhurt." What was "real" life? Father and daughter had two very different responses to the question. For the father, real life was horizontal: the train and telegraph were brought to Amherst, contracts were signed, men were connected to one another, and all of that, to the rhythm of their exchanges, caused wealth to grow. For the daughter, real life was vertical: a movement from the soul to the soul's master—for which there was no need of a railroad. Our only commerce is with the heavens, glowing above our heads and in the depths of our restraint. In such commerce there is nothing to be gained, only a heightened sensitivity to the dried blood of Christ on the breast of a robin, as well as an understanding that grows ever sharper, and therefore ever more painful, of the behavior of other people.

A day comes when no one is a stranger to you anymore. That terrible day marks your entry into real life.

ONE DAY AT NOON, AT THE dinner table, Edward asked
ironically, several times over, if it was "necessary" for an almost
imperceptibly chipped plate to be placed before him. The third
time he asked, Emily rose abruptly to her feet, took the plate, and
smashed it to pieces on a stone in the garden: thy will be done,
our father who cannot bear the sight of a single flaw in matter or
in souls. Another day, outside the stable, Edward was covered in
sweat, his eyes bulging, as he whipped one of his horses until it
bled. He reproached it with a "lack of humility." Emily ran over,
her hair flying, and she screamed at the torturer; he dropped
his whip and stepped back, astounded. A saint's anger is more
terrible than the devil's.

Edward was walled up alive, like all men of Duty. Emily was aware
of the dreariness of his state, and far from holding it against
him, she tried to distract him. It was initially for his sake that
she played the piano and baked bread for the family, a bread
so delicious that it might seem, as she broke it in two, that she
was opening her heart. Her father praised its flavor, would eat
no other, and perhaps when chewing on a savory morsel of his
daughter's bread he had a fleeting glimpse of the child's paradise
that a carefree life could bring.

The morning after her father's funeral Emily wandered like a lost
child through the big, cold house, crying as she entered each
room: "Where is he? Emily will find him!" For two years, she
dreamt of him every night and wrote poems so ardent that their
light could be seen in the beyond—where there were no longer
any roles to be played, nor positions to be held.

ONE MORNING AT THE DICKINSON RESIDENCE, prayer time, just before breakfast: the mother, kneeling, whispered to Emily, also kneeling, that it was so cold she felt she was turning into an "ice floe." Suddenly the father's voice soared, a royal eagle, imposing his silence on everyone else. Edward gleefully listed his children's latest sins, then he read the psalm for the day. His prayers for the souls of his family caused the window panes to rattle as if with "a rain of comets." The scene was so lovely that the mother wiped away a tear with a corner of her linen apron. They sat down to breakfast. The angels' handmaiden took little sips of chocolate from a cup of blue-and-white porcelain from China, with a golden rim. She saw everything, noted everything.

One Sunday afternoon at tea-time: the father was in a foul mood, his silence that of a tomb. The mother and her two daughters were terrified to see him like that. Emily was in charge of opening the door when the bell rang. Slowly the drawing room filled with notables. The father was no more than a torrent of silence in the depths of a leather armchair and Emily, heroically, tried to feed a flagging conversation. She talked about the weather. "I never witnessed such marvelous unanimity." Again, silence. Recalling the morning's sermon, she compared the minister to another one who had died long before and, she explained, she had "never so much as seen the ashes of that gentleman." Again the bell at the front door; it was her cousin Hadley. She was wearing the "furs and robes of her ancestors." And so it went. Like a little girl of twenty-two, Emily watched the adults pile up like logs in the room, each one wearing an expression of springtime mourning. The little girl swayed from one foot to the other, hesitated between terror and laughter. At last the father "adjourned to the kitchen fire" and invited all the dead to follow him. Emily, left on her own, started to write the chronicle of that Sunday for her brother, who was away from home. Her laughter was a rope ladder, unwinding madly from the sky.

EMILY'S MOTHER'S FACE LOOKED AS IF it had been furrowed by a potter's fingers. Her cheeks were thin, her eyes were damp, and her hair poured lankly down either side of her face like black mud. On her breast she wore a silver brooch inlaid with enameled flowers: a rose, a daisy, some primroses. Above the rose a dove spread its wings. Every time Emily looked at her mother she saw this brooch. The brilliance of flowers on a ravaged mother's breast consoled the child for the unending spectacle of melancholy.

Parents see children, never souls. Emily's soul fit in a dew drop. Her realm was the infinitesimal. She contemplated the sky through the stained-glass wings of a firefly, she joined a béguinage in the bell of a lily of the valley. Stars fell from the sky into her hearth, her bed was covered with snow, and her table was made of cherry. Her room had the princely austerity of a monk's cell, and it was all the more beautiful for its discretion.

When all around her ambition was trumpeting, and everyone wanted to be something, she had the sovereign dream of becoming nothing, of dying unknown. Humility was her pride, self-effacement her triumph. In 1856, when her mother opened the floodgates to her illness, Emily dreamt of a world so humble that death might never find its way in: "[…] for I am but a simple child, and frightened at myself. I often wish I was a grass, or a toddling daisy, whom all these problems of the dust might not terrify."

IN 1840 THE DICKINSONS MOVED HOUSE. They would find a refuge for their terrors in a house built all of wood to the north of Amherst, adjacent to the village cemetery. From her window Emily could gaze for hours at the peaceful village of tombstones. Silence and forgiveness wandered along its paths. It was the reflection of paradise in a puddle of water. She watched every funeral, scrutinized the vacant faces behind the burning coffin. The living and their dead came in together through the main entrance to the cemetery. Then, after a few weightless words that drifted with melancholy like children's balloons into the blue sky, the living went away again, leaving their dead to a new life.

In 1855 the family was able at last to buy what had been their first house. This second—and ultimate—move was soul-wrenching to Emily, but she found the grace to smile about it. "I believe my 'effects' were brought in a bandbox, and the 'deathless me' on foot, not many moments after." From the age of ten to twenty-four she had been happy, living in the house overlooking the tombstones. She would always speak of it as "her" house, whereas the other one, where she was born and where she would die, was "my father's house." No sooner did they return to that house than Edward had a cupola built for the roof, and its eight windows provided an outlook toward the approaching enemy—in other words, almost anyone who was not a Dickinson.

FROM ONE SIDE, THE HOUSE WHERE she was born looked out onto the busy main street, and from the other, onto the ecstatic face of the Everlasting: an orchard offered the inspired poetry of its fruit trees; the prose of a kitchen garden was set out in rows like spelling tests, marked with the red ink of a strawberry bush; the Bible of a meadow—pages flung wide, illuminated with daisies and buttercups—was studied all day long by hundreds of theologian butterflies. Emily's father had built her a greenhouse, a narrow glass chapel where she could converse with rare flowers in deepest winter.

Emily had two tables where she liked to write: one in her bedroom, the other in the drawing room. In the drawing room a honeysuckle bush pressed its arabesques against the windowpane, and in summer, birdsong from the rowan tree entered the open window of her bedroom overlooking the meadow, to bless her writing. The poems set on paper gave off the same golden light as the wheat gathered into haystacks. This could not be heaven—for it to be heaven, one must be dead. It was something like heaven, reassuring, deceiving.

All through Emily's early childhood the Dickinson family were merely tenants in one part of the brick house. The other part was inhabited by the owner, a hat manufacturer, Deacon David Mack. The Dickinson children were terrified by his hoary lion's head, his burning blue eyes, his virtuous stiffness, convinced as they were, several times a day, that it was God in a stovepipe hat they saw coming into the house. In spite of such a neighbor, the early years were filled with trust. Emily's mother warned her not to go alone to the nearby woods; she could be bitten by snakes, poisoned by flowers, kidnapped by a sorcerer. The child learned of these dangers and was filled with wonder. She escaped, let her mind wander, came back, reported she had seen "nothing but angels" who were even more intimidated by their encounter than she was.

We all make a home of our own unhappiness. Emily spent her childhood not so much in any house built of brick or wood as in such a home, which although it did not exist was altogether too present. The brooch sparkled on her mother's thin chest. The rare smiles of the goddess were unforgettable. "Two things I have lost with Childhood—the rapture of losing my shoe in the Mud and going Home barefoot wading for Cardinal flowers and my mother's reproof which was more for my sake than her weary own for she frowned with a smile..."

ON THE FARM WHERE SHE GREW UP, in Monson, Emily's mother found her little brother dead in his cradle, like a little sugar loaf wrapped up by death the grocerwoman. Then she lost two other brothers and her father. Finally, one year before Emily's birth, she buried her mother. She brought her daughter into the world under a sun spotted with mourning. A few days before giving birth she repapered the walls of the nursery, but it is not enough to redecorate the walls to ensure a newborn child of an open life. Ghosts bent over Emily's cradle. They observed this child who would become their scribe; her radiant sensibility already permeated the wall of inattention that divides absent from present.

Poets are pretty when a century has gone by, when they're dead and in the ground and alive through their texts. But when you have a poet in your home, a child who is in love with the absolute, shut away in her room with her books like some young wild animal in a divinely smoke-filled lair, how are you to raise her? Children know all there is to know of heaven until the day they begin to learn things. Poets are children who have not been interrupted; they are sky-gazers, impossible to raise.

Legend has it that Saint Christopher carried the Christ child across a river on his shoulders. The truth is that it is mothers who step bare-legged into the great black current of time, carrying their children on their shoulders, feeling the corset of cold around their waists, and they think only of keeping the child above water. Sometimes one of them lets go and sinks into the river. Then it is up to the child, drenched to the soul in fear, to become the mother of her mother and try to reach the opposite shore. From 1850 on, Emily's mother's brain was on fire. She became the prophetess of a migrainous God, and her silent oracles caused her entourage to tremble. Emily looked after her mother. She bustled about in the middle of the black river, not without a certain cheer when she spoke of that time in her late childhood when her mother dressed her in cloth so poorly cut that she felt as if she were "wearing excuses rather than clothing." In 1880— for thirty years she had been carrying her on her shoulders—she let out a sigh: "the cricket of the hearth is a burden, because it is getting old."

MELANCHOLY MOTHERS CAN NEVER BE thanked enough. Their throne is in the middle of the sky. They have tossed their shawl over the sun. From their eyes comes a night so deep that their children marvel at the tiniest spot of light. Emily went in search of daylight where it could be found, not far from the realm of mothers—in passionate nighttime discussions with her brother, for example, by the hearth in the kitchen with its apple-green walls, "while the righteous sleep."

When he had finished his studies, Austin left for Boston to become a teacher and was beset with homesickness—although that home was nothing more than a brick house in Amherst, and that house nothing more than his mother's slow-beating heart. He came back to Amherst, and his father offered him a job. He accepted. His mother observed her son's return in silence. Silence is the sword of moody mothers. They plunge it into the nomad souls of their shattered children. Blessed are the mothers: whoever makes life impossible for us gives our heart every chance to become great.

With his disheveled ginger hair and turned out like a prince—a brightly colored riding jacket, a wide-brimmed planter's hat, an orangewood walking stick—Austin strode up and down the streets of Amherst like a monarch in his tiny kingdom. He was the treasurer at the college, and like his father before him he decided upon the spirit of the education to be dispensed there. He liked painting, theatre, and horses. Swaggering and scathing, he was curt with everyone except Emily. His sister fascinated him. For him she was the "incarnation of good." He needed her, even once he was married. Emily joked with him, mended his socks and shirts, asked him to go shopping for her, pressed him for the town gossip. She flattered, reassured, and encouraged him. She was his little mother. Emily watched over Austin, and Vinnie watched over Emily. The three children held hands and tried to cross the great river of life without drowning. They had no parents. No one has ever had parents, someone whose mere presence could keep one from dying—that does not exist.

LIKE THE WIND IN THE ASPEN LEAVES, life wrote its luminously contradictory texts on the face of Sophia Holland, Emily's friend. Suddenly God creased the masterpiece of that adolescent face as if it were paper. When Emily learned that her friend was going to die, she asked to see her. Death is a potter spinning his work backward. Emily observed the body's clay, its divine breath departing. That vision would make her forever the custodian of vanished lives, a dealer in stolen invisibility. Sophia's soul dropped like an emerald into the jewel box of her red heart.

As a child, Emily heard a minister—thunderstruck by his own eloquence like a horseman thrown by his mount—exclaim: "Is the arm of our Lord so short that He can save no one?" The minister replied dully to his own question, yet he could not put out the fire lit in a child's mind. Sophia buried, Emily entered the convent of depression on tiptoe. To help her recover, her parents sent her to her aunt Lavinia's for a month. For the second time she would find peace there, even if she could not forget Sophia's lesson: with every second, behold the end of the world.

Love and the void belong to the same terrible genus. Our soul is the terrain of their unsettled contest.

WHENEVER A YOUNG MAN SHOWED AN interest in the Dickinson daughters, their father would raise the Great Wall of his eyebrows, but he could not prevent Joseph Lyman from charming the sleek, witty, flirtatious Vinnie. The young man kissed her by her rosebushes then vanished, on the pretext that Vinnie could not have borne the thought of leaving her family home. Vinnie remained petrified among her roses, as if in a fairy tale, frozen in the fateful moment of a curse.

The rosebush deserter vanished into the distance. Beneath his horse's hooves was stardust, the golden powder of a vision, a portrait of Emily that he would write in 1860: "A library dimly lighted [. . .] Enter a spirit clad in white, figure so draped as to be misty[,] face moist, translucent alabaster, forehead firmer as of statuary marble." "Hazel" eyes that do not see what appears before them but "the core of all thi[n]gs"; "hands small, firm, deft but utterly emancipated from all claspings of perishable things, very firm strong little hands, absolutely under control of the brain [. . .] mouth made for nothing and used for nothing but uttering choice speech, rare thoughts, glittering, starry misty figures, winged words."

In her lifetime, Emily would not see her forehead circled in a crown of genius; all her writing would sleep at the bottom of a drawer in her night table, along with her crown of thorns. While she wrote, Vinnie fed the cats that followed her every-where through the house—little gold-eyed courtesans for a lady in black cashmere. She also swept the steps and did the shopping. She played the role of Martha in the Gospel; she had the sententious toughness for it. "[Emily] had to think—she was the only one of us who had that to do. Father believed; and mother loved; and Austin had Amherst." As her sister no longer left the house, Vinnie acted as her dressmaker's dummy, trying on the seraphic white dresses that Emily would wear. When shopkeepers asked her why she did not try to convince her sister to get some fresh air "for her own good," she replied that Emily was gifted for a fervent life of reading and silence. Why on earth should she oblige her to do anything else?

DURING THE NIGHT ON INDEPENDENCE DAY, 1879, a large warehouse in the center of town not far from the Dickinson home went up in flames. The bells woke Emily, and she ran barefoot to the window, saw a giant sun devouring the sky while a pale moon looked on in astonishment. Drawn from their nests by the disaster, drunk on light, the birds were singing full-throated. Vinnie ran in and immediately reassured her sister. "Don't be afraid, Emily, it's only the fourth of July!" She took her by the hand and led her to their mother's bedroom. The din had not awoken her. She was one of those souls who were so unhappy that nothing could trouble them; such indifference is not unlike wisdom. The two daughters let her sleep. Maggie, the housekeeper, was sitting by her side. She in turn reassured Emily: it was only a barn burning, nothing more. Emily acted as if she believed their lies. On Amherst's main street the witches in the fire combed their long red hair, biting ravenously into the wood. Outside it was so light that one could make out a caterpillar's velvet accordion on the leaf of a plum tree at the end of the garden. "Vinnie's 'it's only the fourth of July' I shall always remember. I think she will tell us so when we die, to keep us from being afraid."

There were four windows in Emily's room—and a fifth one, the Bible, a picture window through which the soul discovered a paradise, terribly near. Emily's Bible, in fine-grained green morocco leather, was printed in such tiny characters that she had to hold it very close to her face to read it. In one of the stories, three children were thrown into the flames. They were found sitting around the fire, laughing and singing praises. No doubt they had an invisible Vinnie by their side to help them pass through the flames of abandonment, with a peace in their soul that nothing could wrest from them.

"My country is Truth," said Emily, and referring to her sister's lingering migraines, "Vinnie lives much of the time in the State of Regret." She who was so gifted at bringing tranquility to her loved ones was powerless against this nostalgia for a stolen kiss by the flaming rosebush.

JEALOUS SERPENTS GLIDED ACROSS THE FLOOR of the room where the three little Dickinsons walked barefoot: by day they lurked in the shadows of the children's games, by night they rippled among the tall grasses of a dream. Thirty years later they were still there. There were times when Austin rebelled against his sister's invisible consecration. He claimed that she was "posing" when she received guests—dressed in a cloud of white, speaking to them in a little girl's voice. But if anyone tried to make him admit to his sister's strangeness he clenched his jaw; she went so rarely into the streets of Amherst that people called her "The Myth." There is nothing odd about my sister's behavior, he would affirm, rebuffing strangers who were unaware that the Dickinson clan was a law unto itself. Vinnie said as much, haughtily, "Each of us in this family is the king of his or her own realm."

Edward had gagged his soul to such a degree that—like a revenge of the invisible—the children he had fathered were daydreamers, devourers of books. Austin had become a jurist, yet he showed Emily a few poems of his own devising. She read them and remarked, with an iron humor: "Now Brother Pegasus, I'll tell you what it is—I've been in the habit *myself* of writing some few things, and it rather appears to me that you're getting away my patent, so you'd better be somewhat careful, or I'll call the police!" Brother Pegasus would abandon his writing, at least with ink. At his own expense, he redesigned the grounds of the college, planting bushes with red berries to warm the winter, and trees that retained their green confidence all through the gray months. This goodness that seeks no reward for itself, this restlessness for the faraway are marks of deepest poetry.

IN THE GLOOM OF THE LITTLE SCHOOL, Emily discovered the power of books to resurrect. In high school she fell in love with a young teacher, Leonard Humphrey. He died in 1851. The Lord burning behind a beloved face gives it his brilliance. If he comes too close, the face turns waxy white, then melts and disappears. "I do not care for the body—I love the timid soul, the blushing, shrinking soul."

The pupil of Amherst, too well-behaved, watched as God made up the world with each passing instant. She compiled a secret list of what she loved: poets, the sun, summer, paradise. That was all. The list was full, she wrote, and the word "poets" would suffice in itself: poets give birth to a sun more pure than the sun itself, their summer never fades, and heaven can only be a place of beauty if a poet has painted it.

FIERCE, SILENT, PRONE TO FITS OF LAUGHTER, Emily belonged to a small group at her high school, each of whom had a nickname. Hers was "Socrates"—for the thinker who exasperated the people of Athens with his stubborn pursuit of the truth. The girls addressed impatient letters to each other and several times a day hid behind their fans of pealing laughter. They knew that the more serious days of harvest time lay ahead: husband, children, respectability. Emily sipped delicately at the wine of youth, at the ephemeral grace where sorrows and fervor can be shared. Disappointment arrives from on high. The time would come for them to leave, but for whom, and why?

Something is given at birth to each newborn child. This thing is nothing; it has neither shape nor name nor prestige. It is our only asset. We glimpse it in flashes. "I find ecstasy in life; the mere sense of living is joy enough." Saints share this white flower of nothingness that blooms from time to time in a red heart. It never fades. To be a saint is to be alive. To be alive is to be oneself, one of a kind. Abiah Palmer Root—sensual, radiant, upright—climbed the stairs with the solemn slowness of a queen to where Emily was waiting, astonished. Abiah was a vision: in her hair, and dangling like trophies from her ears, were flaming dandelion flowers. Her peasant grace and her triumphant calm fractured Emily's heart. Until 1854 Emily would address her in writing as the Mother Superior of the Order of Dandelions.

Abiah did not know that she was a vision. She did not always reply, at the risk of ending up in the "box of Phantoms," where Emily put those who disappointed her. As she learned the weaknesses of the world, Emily discovered in return the force of writing. That girl who had once made earrings from the tousled sunlight of dandelions moved on, elsewhere, into a life that was dimmed and comfortable. The glory of dandelions has remained: even in the torment of lashing autumn rains, or grazed by cows hobbled to a monotonous hunger, these flowers radiate the language that knows how to express them and love them. The word is an imperishable sun.

EMILY'S TIME AT AMHERST ACADEMY was over. A party was held to celebrate, a few speeches lightened by a young girls' choir. Emily was a member of the chorus. They sang, those virgins of Amherst. They chirped. No one noticed that in the midst of the choir of sparrows there was a robin: Emily.

The angel of conversion was knocking around the region. You could see him lurking, wooden sword in hand, in Mount Holyoke, outside the walls of the seminary where Emily was enrolled for further study. There were three hundred girls here, pecking at the seeds of knowledge under the pale light of daily sermons. The mother hen, Mary Lyon, kept an eye on everyone, identified the shakier souls among them. One day the pupils were asked to get up from their chairs to testify that they belonged to the new Church, and they all obeyed except for Emily. The angel of conversion, alerted by a tumult of jealous reproach, arrived on the scene, looked at the young rebel on her chair, and voiced his diagnosis: no use insisting, that one won't change. Her coffin will be made of the same wood as her cradle. All societies colonize heaven. Emily did not want to belong to any of them, particularly the association of the friends of God. If God wanted to come, he would know where to find her. Let the good pupils go to their fine ceremonies. Saints are not good pupils.

Emily stayed only a few months at Mount Holyoke. Her father's desire to have his daughter back at home put an end to her studies. When she arrived, they were all "at the door to welcome the returned one, from mother, with tears in her eyes, down to pussy, who tried to look as gracious as was becoming her dignity." Then the house closed around her like an oyster around its pearl. She would never get away from it again. "Home is the definition of God"—and God would not tolerate any absences.

IN THE OPULENT DICKINSON RESIDENCE, which six Irish servants struggled to maintain, night slipped in and came to sniff at those souls imperceptibly wrested by sleep from their bodies. Everyone was asleep; there was no sound save the miserly ticking of a clock—a guillotine of seconds—and, from time to time, the creaking of an old oak wardrobe (there was nothing to be done for such sylvan rheumatism). Night crept upstairs, where Emily's mother, lashed all day long by melancholy, welcomed it like a blessing; Emily's father celebrated it like a promotion, now that at last he could unburden his shoulders of a sackful of social conventions heavier than a dead donkey. Night went back down the stairs, was about to enter the drawing room, then recoiled from a brightness of candles: it was Emily, playing the piano. Soon she would stop in order to write until late at night—not that that would keep her from being the first one up in the morning to make breakfast for everyone.

Everything that was alive about church—the babbling flames of candles, the heart's exaltation for those who were absent, the miraculous dismissal of the mercantile world—she adopted as her own. She borrowed scansion from the psalms to play the piano. Before she sat down at her instrument, she laid a cloth over the upper and lower octaves, in order to recreate the sound of her very first piano, on which she had learned to play "The Grave of Bonaparte" and "Maiden, Weep No More." She played those popular tunes at the age of fourteen, then left them behind and began to improvise. She titled one of her compositions "The Devil." Those who heard it found it strange. In the Bible, the devil is known as "the accuser." Emily's task was just the opposite: she would be the ultimate defender of all that was most luminously fragile in life. And she dedicated the tune to the shadow that remained. Even if she sometimes called herself the "daughter of Satan"—pretending to be sorry she could not join her friends as they flocked to God and Mary Lyon, entrusting them with the key to their dreams—one could hardly hear anything more than an angelic amusement in this mischief of notes deep in the night. Everything must breathe and sing in us, even nothingness.

It was at Aunt Lavinia's that she first discovered the purpose of a piano: to fend off, through playing—even with the trembling little hands of a lost child—the unbearable sorrow of knowing one has been abandoned. A piano can shelter you from a storm, as can the page of a pure book. For a time Emily dreamt of becoming a pianist, until a recital in Boston by Anton Rubinstein dissuaded her; she would never manage to attain that level of excellence in music. After the concert she immersed herself once and for all in the gold-bearing seam of writing. Henceforth the piano would be little more than a nocturnal stroll around the prison yard—a few moments to emerge from the cell of one's mind, to place one's fingers carefully upon the keyboard, like pressing a grain into the soil.

The night had found its queen: there was someone in the Dickinson household who almost never slept. Awkward flowers opened to the air at two o'clock in the morning. No one complained, not even the Dickinsons' guests, often roused from their sleep by the "devil's" lament.

POETRY IS MORE THAN JUST a manner of writing; it is a way of finding one's bearings, turning one's life to the rising sun of the invisible. The gingerbread that Emily baked, and that she lowered from her room in a basket on the end of a rope to the children waiting in the street; the stubborn care she devoted to her rosebushes; her winged patience in the face of her mother's tyrannical languor—everything, for Emily, was an opportunity to display the empathy that was the clear source of genius. And no sooner did Susan arrive on the scene than she was taken into the enchanted circle of Emily's solicitude.

Susan's father had been the keeper of a disreputable tavern in Amherst. Tuberculosis had deprived her of a mother when she was nine. Cheap wine would take her father two years later. Sooner or later everyone is called upon to enter the house of the ogre. In little Susan's life, the ogre was a draper, the husband of one of her sisters, and Susan thought she would find shelter with them. The draper looked down on her for being dependent on him. Every morning she saw herself, in his eyes, as coarse—as if the stains of sediment that had darkened her father's apron, that man dazed with ignorance, were now visible on her own soul. As soon as she could, she left and went into service, lodged in insalubrious rooms, gazed at the holes in her socks, and discovered books, which would teach her that nothing is ever finished, since with each new reading she would find a text as pure as the snow fallen with the night.

At the age of twenty Susan was a dark beauty, with laughter to horsewhip misfortune. Austin embarked on a hesitant courtship. Emily was fascinated by the young woman and spread the rumor that her brother was "engaged." The village rippled with the news, and Austin eventually relented: he married this woman, and for several months she would refuse to engage with him in what she referred to as the "base practices of marriage." Harsh, impatient, ambitious, she was perfect. To win the love of such a woman was like having a mother's attention all to oneself—an impossible, thrilling task.

All marriages are subtle alloys of death and resurrection. Through marriage, Susan went from a slandered father who rolled his casks full of the red devil to a father-in-law to whom the white marble angels of notability bowed low. Edward commissioned an Italianate villa of ginger wood for the young couple, called the Evergreens, across the street from Emily's house of orange brick. There were a hundred yards between the two houses. For the next thirty years, along the smuggler's path that joined them, there would be a traffic of books, flowers, medication, eggs, words of love, and words of farewell—which are the stormy variant, and more convincing in their way, of words of love.

HENCEFORTH, ON SEEING SUSAN OR READING her name in the newspaper, no one would catch a whiff of the fug of stale wine and wet dog in which her father had lived and was buried. The golden honeysuckle trumpets, the heat-heavy roses outside the Evergreens, and the Dickinsons' indisputable wealth gave off a more worthy odor. Susan endeavored to enlarge her world. Her guests—gentlemen of the law, politicians, writers on the lecture circuit—clustered like hornets beneath the lantern by the entrance, bewitched by their hostess's dark eyes, subjugated by her severity, her red Indian shawls, the silver bracelets jangling on her wrist. Emily watched from her room, where one window overlooked the Evergreens, as the great and good went up the granite steps. The acclaimed writers of her era—the likes of Emerson, renowned thinker of the invisible, who came to stay the night with Austin and Susan—were unaware that they had gone to the wrong entrance, and that the greatest poet of the century was just there, in the house next door, behind a curtain of trembling lace.

When too much vanity rose to her sister-in-law's lips, Emily put everything right again in a letter, and on the cheek of the paper there was a sudden bruise: "Your Riches—taught me—Poverty."

FROM SUSAN EMILY LEARNED THE SUPERNATURAL
inadequacy of all love. In return, she brought her the breadth of
life that can be gained by thinking about it, writing about it. She
showed Susan her poems. One of them evoked the dead in the
waiting room of resurrection—their "alabaster chambers"—and
after Susan critiqued it, Emily rewrote it. In the poems Susan
was called, among other things, Cleopatra, Goliath, Vesuvio,
Eternity—and, in three erotic poems, Captain Dobbin. Susan's
genius was to let a thousand endearments come her way, without
ever rejecting a single one but without ever really responding,
either. Emily's soul was sparked by this absence of an echo, like
a child who from her darkened room calls to her mother in vain
and is finally dazzled by her own tears.

In June 1852 Emily wrote to Susan, who was staying in Baltimore
at the time, and slipped some violets into the letter. The mailman
was Emily's own father, who was passing through Baltimore on
the way to his party convention. Edward supposed he was deliv-
ering a young girl's letter, something nebulous and pointlessly
trivial. He was blinded by his Puritanism. The master of Amherst
was holding a few sheets of burning gold in his hands; on the
envelope protecting them were these penciled words: "Open me
carefully."

Susan gave birth to three children, in spite of herself. The first-
born, Ned, was epileptic, as if the trembling fear of poverty that
his mother had buried deep in her soul had returned to convulse
her son's flesh. Austin named one of the horses in his stable for
the boy; the supple, bright bay offered some consolation for the

sorrow of engendering a child who shivered like autumn's dry leaf on the end of its branch. This birth would bring about a first, only faintly perceptible distancing—breath on a mirror—from Emily. Her letters continued to beat their wings outside Susan's window—thousands of words endowed with an imperious life; lofty, imploring words.

Each of Susan's journeys left Emily in a fever of words: "[. . .] when you go away. I'll keep you in a casket—I'll bury you in the garden—and keep a bird to watch the spot." Naturally, that would be pointless: no ties can remain frozen in time, even those we bind with the dead.

The love between the two women must fracture, irresistibly, but the golden vase, even cracked, could still hold the water of a limpid word. One day Emily learned that Susan came to the house without asking to see her, and she cried out, "I would have come out of Eden to open the Door for you if I had known you were there."

AMHERST WAS A COCOON, THREE THOUSAND inhabitants in a plain watched over by an uncompromising forest of fir trees. To Susan it was a mere wilderness, for she loved nothing more than to get away to New York to buy black sequined gowns, which were all the fashion in 1860. In a poem, Emily compared two sorts of victors. There are those who have the world's acclaim, who enjoy sparkling gowns, opera concerts, and exhilarating voyages; then there are those who triumph over the world by succumbing to its force: they are the ones who stay at home, proudly cloaked in snow. In the large towns around Amherst, piano recitals blossomed and faded in the course of an evening. Emily had no more liking for such evenings out than her father did. The most astonishing thing about a spectacle, she said, was the spectators themselves. Nothing happened in Amherst, and that nothing was life in its purest form. Susan sought the admiration of society, and Emily found nourishment in the sky; between them, the distance grew, a chill settled in. The golden vase froze and shattered. Emily gathered up the pieces in her heart, but for sixteen years she would not return to the house next door.

To describe Amherst, which to Emily was a sacred town, Susan called it a "staring, lonely, hopeless place, enough to make angels homesick. The lugubrious sound of the church bell still rings in my Winter dreams." The tone is bitter. The woman speaking was elderly; she had come to the end of her performance, most of the actors had already left the stage, and in the front row there sat only a few astonished dead people. Austin—nicknamed "the rooster" in his youth—had been deceiving her for years with a woman who was more cheerful. Death had taken the sweetest of their three children. Amherst despised Susan in equal measure, bestowing on her the reputation of a flirt and a drunkard, the same woman whom Emily, in spite of their estrangement, had always seen as "shy and without stain." Death would come for Susan and lay her in its herbarium. The years passed over the names of those people, effaced the prominence of their complaints, caused their devotion to shine.

EMILY'S GRAVE, ONLY RECENTLY SEALED, had become a battlefield. Once the stupor of sorrow, impossible to simulate, had passed, the family read her poems, pen in hand. Vinnie would scratch through the poem addressed to Susan, "One Sister have I in our house / And one, a hedge away," and remove its dedication. Another poem, in which Emily dreamt of weeping on Susan's breast, was reassigned to a minister's wife, a woman above suspicion. But Emily's voice, invincible with purity, removed her friend from hell: in the gravel lane bordered by hollyhock between the two Dickinson houses, a transfigured Susan would appear, braving censure and death, rubbing her hands to banish a wine stain that she alone could see.

"Should I turn in my long night I should murmur 'Sue.'" A song rises, filtered through poetry. It seeks to speak what is pure, what is true. Books preserve the living song after the death of the singer, but poetry does not settle only in books. Sometimes it goes by without a sound, like the angel of the everyday whom no one sees. The gingerbread for the children, the pillow plumped beneath her mother's rambling head were more pure, more real than anything.

EMILY'S MOTHER ALWAYS SPOKE IN a low voice. Books intimidated her. The people around her reminded her that she was uneducated, and her indifference to writing became one of those family jokes beneath which a family member can be buried alive with great shovelfuls of laughter. They all tended to be scathing in that family, except for her. Can one survive without ever being cruel? It does not prevent one from having a poetical—precise, that is—view of reality. She told Emily how at the funeral of Jennie Hitchcock a hen and her chicks tried to jump up and fly through the window onto the dead woman's bed. Now that the canvas had been prepared, Emily filled it with her colors: I suppose, said she, that the hen and her chicks wanted to say their farewells to the woman who used to feed them. From the age of twelve Emily had been helping her mother in the garden and shared her love for naïvely colored anemones. Later, as she bent over a blank page, she learned to transform maternal melancholy into compassion for all the lost lives.

In 1875 an attack of paralysis would leave Mrs. Dickinson utterly dependent on her daughter. The gentleness that enveloped them had not existed in such a pure form until now. Then came the death sentence in 1882. When we are about to lose everything, something inside, in the pit of our stomach, warns us, a two-hundred-ton haystack falling from the sky into our guts. Emily did not attend the funeral. She stayed in her room, seated at her table, looking at the insatiable blueness of the sky. "I cannot tell how Eternity seems. It sweeps around me like a Sea." There are events so powerful that they wrench our brain from our skull.

Heaven is the place where we will no longer need reassurance.

EMILY KNEW SOMETHING THAT THE OTHERS did not know. She knew that we will never love more than a handful of people, and that at any time this handful can be blown away by the innocent breath of death, like the feathers of a dandelion clock. She also knew that writing is the angel of resurrection.

After her aunt Lavinia's death in 1860, Emily grew closer to Lavinia's daughters, Louise and Frances. She called them "her children" and sent them letters as densely populated as dolls' houses. Each letter raised the curtain of ink on a scene that was either funny or cruel—like the day when an old lady asked Emily to help her find her way: Emily wrote, "I directed her to the cemetery to save the expense of moving." The Dickinson house was a baroque theatre, and for twenty-six years Emily kept a vivid chronicle of it for her cherished cousins: "[. . .] always I have a chair for you in the smallest parlor in the world, to wit, my heart." The spectacle was always new and radiant, save one time when Emily, tormented by her mother's absence, spoke of an "old nail" piercing her breast.

There is no more difference between the tone of these letters and that of the poems than there is between life and the Eternal. God is the absolute reader. He can decipher with ease both a soul and the Aramean dance of butterflies on a parchment of air, but in his opinion our scriptures are always somewhat stained with the brownish marks of convention—except in Emily's letters to her cousins. There, he can surprise the fantasy of his creation as if in a pocket mirror.

In her struggle to the death with death, Emily often triumphed. In one letter she described her mother coming home of an evening with grass clinging to her shawl, a sure sign of winter's defeat and the victorious advent of spring. A century earlier, Amherst's little theatre had collapsed on all its actors—and yet in Emily's letter, her mother had come home to open the door of the page and enter the reader's soul with the childlike proof of resurrection on her shawl.

HER GARDEN WAS HER ONLY CHURCH. She could not be bothered with theology. She saw how the cool hand of the breeze placed a maternal caress on the fevered brow of the roses, and she offered a conclusion that none of the doctors of the Church would ever have found, for all their cautious erudition: "I believe the love of God may be taught not to seem like bears."

The author of a guidebook to the flowers of North America spoke with equal fervor of the innocence of brambles and the wildness of a sky that no one could enter in their lifetime. Emily was enthralled by the enthusiasm of this visionary gardener. "When Flowers annually died and I was a child, I used to read Dr. Hitchcock's Book on the Flowers of North America. This comforted their Absence—assuring me they lived." Dandelions, their solar caravans paused here and there in the meadows, were her favorite flowers. She picked a clover leaf from her father's grave and pressed it in the Bible, on this verse from the Epistles to the Hebrews: "Now faith is the substance of things hoped for, the evidence of things not seen."

From earliest childhood, and until her time with Mary Lyon, Emily picked the flowers that grew daydreaming in the woods and hills around Amherst. She baptized them with their Latin name, then laid them beneath a blanket of translucent paper in the dormitory of her herbarium, where soon over four hundred pale nuns from another world would be sleeping. On each page several blooms framed the majesty of a central flower, their petals hardly creased, their stems held in place by shining sticky paper. As they waited for the staggering sun of their rebirth, they recalled the luminous breath of their former life.

ONE CLEAR JUNE MORNING IN 1874 the stores in Amherst closed their shutters, while in the sky above the village, half an hour's silence was kept, like the silence of the Apocalypse after the angel had broken the seventh seal of the book. The eye of the hurricane was to be found in the Dickinsons' library: an open casket. Austin suddenly leaned over it and, with the clumsy fervor of a young girl, kissed the granite brow of his dead father. "I would never have dared to do this when you were alive," he said as he straightened up and took three steps back, aghast at his own boldness. The dead man accepted his homage without trembling; the cadaver filled the pillar of society to overflowing, and together they were nothing more than one immense, taciturn rage, icy and powerless. Emily was in her bedroom. She sat at her desk and listened to the voices downstairs, so quiet that she was terrified; she would not go down to gaze at the stone statue.

Two days earlier, June 16, a few hours before her father's frayed heart would shatter from death's blows, Emily found a way to keep her mother and sister at a distance: Edward was due to leave for Boston that afternoon, and she wanted to spend those few hours with him, although she could not know that they would be his last. She stunned her father with her unusual vernal speech. Her gaiety was deafening, like the song of a bird inebriated with its own endlessly repeated call. She did not know what was causing her to speak like that. Only later that evening would she understand that her joy had given her father the vital sustenance for his journey into the beyond. For now, when the wretched hour of his departure arrived, Emily accompanied him to the station. The train pulled out. As if preparing to greet a small child traveling for the first time without his parents, death was waiting for Edward on the incoming platform.

AFTER HER FATHER'S DEATH, AS HER brother would testify, irritably, white became a dogma for Emily: a white dress, white lilies every day—eternal snows on the summits of the spirit. From time to time an Aztec lily, whose reddish-orange tint was better suited to her red hair—a transcendental stylishness.

Every year the door to the Dickinson house opened, and the garden lit up its rosebushes and copses for a reception in honor of the former pupils of the college. The lady in white came down from her lofty chambers to comfort someone's spirit, but finding no one in need of comfort in that noisy assembly, after a few words that were not understood she went back upstairs. Her appearance was merely a prelude to her withdrawal.

Whenever old ladies in the neighborhood called to her in her garden to say hello, she always had a flower or a poem taken out to them on a silver platter, in her place. A flower or a poem: both of these envoys—the first with its nostalgia for light, the second with its science of brevity and wit—were the perfect representatives of a soul in exile.

EMILY'S VOICE—THE ONE THAT EMERGED FROM the golden sarcophagus the moment it was opened—was hurried, the voice of someone who arrives breathless, running toward us from a great distance. A voice full of dashes, condensed clauses: the voice of an asthmatic angel, or of a little girl bringing such incredible news that the words jostle each other in her mouth, so convinced is she that we will not hear her. One evening in August 1870 the asthmatic angel, the little girl whom no one believed, and the feverish lady in white stood before Higginson, who could not believe his eyes.

A former minister, a soldier who had fought for the abolition of slavery, a man of letters with a curiosity about new writing, Higginson had the chalky head of individuals who are convinced they are fighting for a good cause. His soul was placid. When one of his soldiers died at his side, in combat, he wrote to his wife that he "felt nothing more than if it were a tree that had fallen." Emily fell into his reassuring life like a meteorite. In 1862 Higginson published an essay addressed to budding writers in the *Atlantic Monthly*. After reading it, Emily sent him a letter bursting with humility, a star offering to be his pupil; she submitted a few poems and asked him to verify whether they "breathed." Flabbergasted, Higginson asked for information about her person; she responded with information about her soul. Her only companion, she said, was her dictionary. Eight years went by before they first met, in Amherst, eight years freshened by the gusts of Emily's letters.

Through a trapdoor in the heavens of language—which she alone knew how to reach—Emily spilt so much light onto this man sated with literature that he was blinded. She showed him around the ironworks of her mind: her poems were born in response to a "sudden light on orchards, or a new fashion in the wind." Writing was a way to calm the fever of the first morning of the world, a fever that returned with every new day. She also laughed at herself, said that she was "the only kangaroo among the beauty," and with that phrase alone, outclassed all the insipid queens of a day.

A CONFRONTATION WITH THE ICY GOD of the temple or a lurking death on the battlefield might have proven far less trying than coming face to face with Emily, who was wearing a linen dress of "exquisite" whiteness, a shawl of carded blue wool draped over her shoulders. After only a few minutes Higginson was exhausted. Only madness can devour energy to this degree.

Higginson arrived in Amherst in August 1870. He was led into a parlor that was "dark and cool and stiffish." Emily walked toward him in slow motion, a lily in each hand, before suddenly thrusting them at him brusquely. She spoke, her little voice like that of a dying child. She said she knew none of society's codes and apologized timidly, the better to disregard them all. Her words were rash-red from the nettles in the heaven where she walked day and night. When the affable Higginson worriedly questioned her vow of solitude, she replied that she did not miss society at all, of any kind: life was merely a cloth of meditation she must smooth out each day in order to explore its radiant pattern. She placed thought at God's right hand and was astonished at how the living showed no astonishment, so ferocious was their appetite for a life without candor.

Some people are so fervently present to themselves that when we are with them we discover, painfully, that we have a soul. Emily showed more attention to her visitor than he had ever shown himself. For the first time in his life he could feel the ocean of his brain pounding against the bony cliffs of his skull. That same evening at the hotel, like a war correspondent gone missing on the front of the Eternal, he jotted down his notes about this encounter that had left him feeling so exhausted. Intelligence does not consist in setting up an original little shop. Intelligence consists in listening to life and gaining its trust. Never in his life would Higginson be more intelligent than on that night of August 16, 1870, as he wrote down what he had just heard and could scarcely believe. All evening his spirit trembled. His hand on the page was the needle of the seismograph, recording every tremor of the invisible. Emily was at the epicenter of the seism, its miraculous, unbearable cause.

"If I read a book [and] it makes my whole body so cold no fire can ever warm me I know *that* is poetry. If I feel physically as if the top of my head were taken off, I know *that* is poetry. These are the only way I know it. Is there any other way." Higginson had no answer. He had never imagined that poetry might be a vital matter, the apotheosis of all lucidity, the tearing away of the blindfold that life placed over the eyes of the living to allay their fear of that final moment, which was every passing moment.

EMILY'S COUNTRY WAS BORDERED BY THE hedge surrounding her garden. On the other side of the hedge was a foreign land—America. A brutal, naïve country, draped in a night-blue sky, its stars threatened with extinction by a civil war. That country did not appear often in Emily's writings. She did not belong to that world, did not want its war or its peace. She stared into the eyes of the dead; she contemplated everything with never-ending astonishment.

Absence becomes a breach in the great wall of the world—an in-draft, to which writing responds. One day young Austin, who at the time was away at school, wrote to say he would be coming home for a visit. His mother laid the table, set it ablaze with candles and roses, and prepared his favorite dish, a custard pie (difficult to make on a day when the hens were not laying, but nothing stops a mother's love). The hours went slowly by, the candles melted, and the son failed to arrive: he had canceled his voyage without letting anyone know. Emily went straight to her mother's heart, surveyed the extent of the disaster, and wrote to her brother. "Nobody moved your chair, but there it stood at the table, until dinner was all done, a melancholy emblem of the blasted hopes of the world."

The world was full and cold like a pebble. Lightning shattered the pebble and freed its spirit: Emily saw an empty chair in the middle of the flames of hell. She wrote flush with what she saw.

She could scribble a poem on the wrapper of the chocolate she used to make a cake, just as she could write in the cool, calm

pantry where she skimmed the milk. More than once she started over, made multiple drafts, spared no effort. Everything must
be on the page, which is the opposite of what occurs at any or-
phanage: no one must ever be abandoned again.

SHE DID NOT CHOOSE TO BE A SEER. This gift was more of a cross to bear than a blessing, and the title "Empress of Calvary" that she gave herself had not been usurped. Something prevented her from living, arising gradually as she neared her twentieth year: a fear of unfamiliar faces, a taste for rambling in the hills, invisible to others. Emily Brontë, of whose works she was fond, was a secret model: she too wandered across the moors with her dog, cooked the family bread, gave her stormy heart to be eaten by ghosts, and only twice did she travel away from the paternal parsonage, all the sooner to return, illuminated.

Hawthorne grew up in a freezing house where no one ever saw anyone else, even at mealtimes. In *The House of the Seven Gables*, an old judge forces his cousin Hepzibah to stay by his side until his dying day. Emily sometimes compared herself to Hepzibah; it was hard not to see Edward in the role of jailor judge. But no one is ever quite as one expects: to calm Emily and encourage her to go out, her father bought her a dog, a Newfoundland she baptized Carlo (the name of a dog belonging to a character in *Jane Eyre*, one of her favorite books).

More and more she felt the need to take her distance from a world whose "eyes are wide open," and before long she went no farther than the house across the street. "Austin and Susan are my crowd." Doctors who do not believe in the existence of the soul would speak today of agoraphobia. Medical jargon exists primarily to reassure doctors, not to throw light on illness. Agoraphobia is the hellish disease of those who do not want to leave heaven.

FOR SEVERAL YEARS EMILY TRAVERSED a dark night that had no name, where she alone suffered the chill. Cape Horn was rounded in 1861. "I had a terror since September, I could tell to none; and so I sing, as the boy does of the burying ground, because I am afraid." The devils of anguish, banished a first time when she was two and a half years old, had now come again to pelt her with stones. She escaped by shutting herself away.

Genius is a response to the impossibility of living, a stag bounding above the herd. By radicalizing what she must endure, she changed its meaning: it was to wage a war to end all wars that she went into the house and up the stairs, and disappeared into her room. It was to be thoroughly alive. The work of a saint is to purify life, to extract the precious stone from its coating of dried mud. In her bedroom, with a little brush dipped in ink, Emily polished the word "life"—the ruby given to all. Against the rising tide of death her poems raised the impassable wall of Beauty.

Her withdrawal, which protected her from people's morbid taste for convention, was a way of taking care of them in spite of themselves: "Distance is the root of gentleness." Life would be nothing without contemplation.

FROM APRIL TO NOVEMBER 1864, and April to October 1865, Emily, fearful for her sight, went to Boston for treatment. During that entire period the doctor prohibited her from reading. She stayed with the Norcross cousins, and in spite of their admiration she yearned for the glade of her room and the sky of her books. When all danger had been averted and the doctor informed her that she could go back to reading, she rushed to her *Antony and Cleopatra*: "He whistled up the fox hounds [...] how my blood bounded!" Back in Amherst, as she opened the door to her room and looked out once again through her windows onto the bountiful sky, she felt herself regaining the essential freedom of being only spirit. There would never again be any outings into the world farther than the garden.

Because she almost never received her visitors in person, and spoke to them only through the door to her room, she unburdened them of their corporality, transforming them into angels whom she knew only through their voices. Voices had always taught her about the state of the world. Through them, like a newborn infant prey to a contemplative terror in the depths of her cradle, she could touch the heavens, without any intermediary; she could touch hell.

In June 1882 a childhood friend came to visit, Emily Fowler Ford, with whom she had been corresponding. Emily did not go downstairs to the hall to see her. They spoke for a long time, invisible to each other, one upstairs, the other downstairs, like two prisoners in neighboring cells, each one preserving for the other the never-ageing face of youth. Then her friend went away again, leaving Emily to her tireless struggle against the Roman legions of death.

TO HAVE A SOUL IS TO have a taste for the absolute, and therefore for loss—a ball of light hurled against the high wall of death, rebounding against one's thoughts. The soul was precisely what Samuel Bowles was fleeing. A journalist, editor of the *Springfield Republican*, he was five years older than Emily. He had a Christlike mane of long brown hair, and his cheeks were covered with a leafy coil of black beard. His eyes shone, mother-of-pearl, in the darkened room of his face like Rembrandt's philosopher in the clarity of his gloomy chambers: one saw nothing else. He used charm the way a scorpion uses its sting, with the speed of instinct. He had a childish fascination with powerful people and reported on their doings in his paper. It was because of Edward's political involvement that he frequented the Dickinsons. But their anxiety, their interiority, made them so very different from him. Samuel and Emily immediately took to each other. The inexplicable reasons for certain ties are the best proof that there is a God who takes great pleasure in bringing people together simply in order to tally the sparks and the blows.

What did Samuel Bowles, this man from the outside world, want? He wanted a life that would be as intense as possible. He was a modern man: he believed that nothing could be more intense than "an event"—something that made a stir, that happened quickly, not to be missed at any price. But an event, more often than not, is merely an epiphany of nothingness, a will-o'-the-wisp swirling over the largest graveyard in the world. And what did Emily Dickinson want, this woman of the interior? She too wanted life to be as intense as possible, but for her that intensity was to be found in a slow and silent life of retirement, on the shaded slope of days, where daisies nodded their heads to the weight of the dew, and the dying gasped for one last breath of air.

No one could be further from Emily than Samuel Bowles—which for her was fortunate, an unhoped-for opportunity to elevate life's luminous sorrow with love.

CONTEMPLATIVES ARE KNOWN FOR THE FACT that they neglect no one. A spirit approaching its own heart will find clustered there a crowd of ordinary little people: the realm of the saint is the realm of the ordinary.

Even when she was overwhelmed by her writing, Emily never stopped worrying about her loved ones. In an 1870 census, she was qualified as "without occupation," thus assigned to the same category as children. In those days she was baking the family's bread, gardening, making preserves, soothing her brother, facilitating her father's life, watching over her mother in her gloom, nurturing the Norcross sisters with her letters, and writing poems that attest to the bustling activity of the invisible within our childish souls. Might we all wish to be qualified thus, "without occupation."

BEHIND THE CLOSED DOOR OF HER ROOM, Emily wrote texts whose halting grace has no equal, except, perhaps, in the crystalline prose of Rimbaud. Like a celestial dressmaker, she grouped her poems in packets of twenty, then sewed and bound them in notebooks she buried in a drawer. "To disappear enhances." Just as she was adopting her white dress, Rimbaud, with the careless fury of youth, abandoned his magical book in a printer's cellar and fled to the stunned East. Beneath the studded sun of Arabia, in the proscribed room in Amherst, two ascetics in love with beauty labored to be forgotten.

In the public realm that was his newspaper, Samuel Bowles gladly accepted submissions from female authors but published Emily only very sparingly, at the very time she was in her most fruitful years. In her poems she often portrayed herself as a boy. To Bowles, who was surprised by how much she knew about growing corn, she replied, "That was Emily when a boy." She often compared herself to Antony, in *Antony and Cleopatra*, who according to Shakespeare "pays his heart / For what his eyes eat only." In 1861 the newspaper published a poem in which, this time, Emily painted herself as a bee: a "little tippler Leaning against the sun," "Inebriate of air" and zigzagging among the "inns of molten blue." The "seraphs swing their snowy hats" before her, and the saints rush to the window to admire her. To speak so joyfully of the open air one must have been a recluse since the dawn of time. The poem was published without the author's name, and two lines were changed to comply with a more conventional rhythm; Emily abandoned any hope that Samuel might be the editor to make a hive of a book from her swarm of poems. She continued to write, the way God delivers acts of kindness—on the quiet, on the sly.

WE DO NOT CHOOSE OUR SAVIOR. In 1877 Bowles came to visit the Dickinsons. He asked to see Emily, but she refused to leave her room. Samuel shouted from the bottom of the stairs: "Emily, you damned rascal! No more of this nonsense! I've traveled all the way from Springfield to see you. Come down at once!" And the miracle occurred. Lazarus emerged, dazzled by daylight. Emily came down the stairs and went into the parlor. She had never seemed so gay, so childlike and vivacious. A few days later, she wrote a letter to Bowles, vibrant with sweetness. Attached to the letter was a poem in which she asserted:

> I have no Life but this—
> To lead it here—
> Nor any Death—but lest
> Dispelled from there—
> Nor tie to Earths to come,
> Nor Action new
> Except through this Extent
> The love of you.

Sometimes someone comes into our life to save us from our personage, which we have ended up confusing with our person. A resurrection of this kind requires two things—boldness and love. Boldness is like the fire that cannot be troubled by any nuances of firewood. Love is a kindness tirelessly maintained. Samuel Bowles had only boldness. The resurrection lasted only one afternoon.

Samuel Bowles the imaginary lover was scarcely more generous than Samuel Bowles the newspaper editor. Avid, terribly distracted, he hardly reacted on reading Emily's letters, despite the many phrases that burned like ice to tell the depths of her hopefulness. Thus when he sailed for Europe to explore new faces, she wrote: "I tell you, Mr. Bowles, it is a Suffering, to have a sea—no care how Blue—between your Soul, and you." Upon his return, at first she refused to see him, then the knot of friendship was tied once again. No longer with the woolen thread of feeling, but with the steel wire of a soul convinced of its native solitude.

Since the man was evasive, she tried to reach him through his wife, Mary, and while Samuel Bowles was in Europe Emily set herself up as his second wife in rank: "Not to see what we love, is very terrible—and talking—does'nt ease it—and nothing does—but just itself. The Eyes and Hair, we chose—are all there are—to us—Is'nt it so—Mary? I often wonder how the love of Christ, is done—when that—below—holds—so." Emily often quoted this remark of Charlotte Brontë's: "Life is so constructed, that the event does not, cannot, will not, match the expectation." It came as a relief to her to realize that she had been giving all her blood to a man who did not want any of it, whose amiable indifference resembled the mysterious smile of the angel of dark hours.

In January 1878 the eyes "we chose" became clouded, lost their shine; they no longer reflected the faces of admiring young women, of notables flushed crimson. Everything would vanish: Samuel Bowles gave up to God a soul whose existence he had scarcely suspected, yet from the watchtower of her room a damned rascal had seen, only too well, its idle beauty.

WITH THE WHIPLASH OF HER WORDS Emily could kill a fly on the tip of the nose of whomever she was speaking with. In the dining room of the Willard hotel, where she sat down to dinner, she was observing the gentleman at the next table, a judge to whom a pudding had just been served. A white-gloved waiter, his face masked by the implacable mixture of scorn and obsequiousness that is the mark of a smart restaurant, bent over the pudding, poured a spoonful of rum over it, and struck a match. The flambé delighted the judge. With one word Emily pricked his puerile wonder: "Oh Sir, may one eat of hell fire with impunity here?" The gentleman failed to understand. He could not know that in that month of February 1855, in Washington—where her father, serving in Congress, had invited her along with Vinnie— Emily had seen what the world is: an abattoir for the soul. One does not need time to see this. The anguish of it suffices.

A few days later the two sisters returned to their nest in Amherst. They made a detour through Philadelphia, where they attended a church service—and the sky with its starry pendant fell on Emily: on hearing a sermon by Charles Wadsworth, she recognized a spirit to rank with her own. God looks on, lets us build our projects—houses of cards—then one unforeseeable day he pounds his fist on the table and everything collapses around us: something, at last, has happened.

THE NEWS THE BIBLE HAWKS IS far more essential than the news to be found in newspapers, since it brings news about the person reading it. Through the practice of meditation the reader's soul leaves itself behind, then walks through the wheat fields of the invisible to read in the columns of heaven all about the glory to come.

Emily mocked the punitive use that the clergy made of the Bible. It was customary at the time to send a Bible to sick people to hasten their recovery, so she sent one to her ailing twenty-one-year-old nephew Ned, who had grown sullen and fierce with Austin. On the frontispiece she inscribed a poem, in which she called sin "a distinguished Precipice." And while the song of Orpheus might hold us captive, that of priests "condemns," and the Bible was written by "faded Men." A poem like this would enchant the reverend Wadsworth. The style of his sermons was lively, paradoxical, unsettlingly fantastical. The orator enjoyed making his listeners smile, all the better to destroy their smiles with a sudden blow. He also knew how to use his deep voice to evoke a God nailed like an owl to the barn door of centuries by violent, cowardly men.

The love of victors is a dubious love. Like Wadsworth scorning the implacability of dogma, Emily loved a defeated God: "When Jesus tells us about his Father, we distrust him [...] but when he confides to us that he is 'acquainted with Grief,' we listen, for that is also an Acquaintance of our own."

THE CRAFTSMAN'S HAND OF THOUGHT, POLISHING
Wadsworth's face, had made him bald, and perched on his flat
nose was a pair of little oval steel-rimmed glasses so that he might
stare calmly into the darkness ahead of him. He was married and
was sixteen years older than Emily. This man, whom a reporter
from the *New York Evening Post* portrayed as a "new lion," was
almost as wild as Emily. At the end of his sermons he fled from
his parishioners and their gushing praise; he did not seek to
befriend his peers; he could not be reached in the morning, for
mornings were devoted to reading and writing. He corresponded
with Emily, went to visit her twice in Amherst, in March 1860
and in August 1880. He confided to her that his life was "full of
dark secrets," and did not reveal a single one. Emily was in love
with his soul, which was like a "Dusk Gem"; she said that "to
know him is life itself," but more than anything she appreciated
his mischief. "Without mischief one does not go to heaven"—
and these two managed to break into heaven more than once.

Charles and Emily: two children sitting on the same bench, de-
ciphering the same text on the blackboard of the starry sky. They
talked about the devil with the same smiling indulgence, one in
a sermon—"Satan, if he were properly reformed, would make
an efficient teacher of morality"—the other in a poem in which
the devil, if only he knew how to be faithful, would be the best
of friends, because he had all the qualities required. They also
liked to borrow from mineralogy the brilliance of its terms. For
Wadsworth, just as a diamond was nothing but a piece of carbon
until it had crystallized, man was nothingness until his thought
had cut his soul like a jewel, where every facet celebrated eternal

light. Similarly, Emily evoked the blissful metamorphosis of her spirit into a diamond, and in the Apocalypse, her bedside book, she often meditated on chapter 21, which she called "the chapter of jewels," heavy with amethysts, topazes, and sapphires, like the pouch of an angelic thief.

Charles and Emily were like two prospectors, shaking the gravel of words in their paper pan, until they found the one that shone gold and did not mislead, its carat that of pure truth.

IN 1882 WADSWORTH DIED, AND HIS soul fell onto the little scale of a diamond merchant God. There is no greater joy than to know someone who sees the same world that we see. It is like learning that we are not insane, after all. "On subjects of which we know nothing [...] we both believe, and disbelieve, a hundred times an Hour—which keeps Believing nimble." To speak endlessly of that which endlessly eludes us is a pleasure compared to which all other pleasures are as nothing. To meet someone, truly meet him—and not simply chat as if there were no dying, ever—is an infinitely rare thing. Love's unchanging substance is a shared intelligence of life. In losing Wadsworth, Emily lost half of heaven. On learning of his death she confided to friends: "He was my shepherd."

PHOTOGRAPHERS ARE THE SERVANTS OF DEATH. The same photographer took portraits of two young women on the same day, two women who had no connection between them—Emily Dickinson and Margaret Aurelia Dewing. Margaret was twenty, Emily seventeen. Margaret was smiling in her portrait. Emily was not. By smiling, Margaret lost her secret. Her smile was mere submission to the mechanical will of the photographer, and it dissolved into nothingness before it even reached us. By yielding nothing to the world, Emily kept God from disappearing.

The photographer asked each of them not to move for several minutes, the time it would take for the image to fix itself on the plate of silvered copper—but the spirit is a child who cannot sit still. If one were hoping for a glimpse of Emily's soul, better to read the letter she wrote to Higginson in July 1862, which flutters like a sparrow in a bush. "Could you believe me without? I had no portrait, now, but am small, like the wren; and my hair is bold, like the chestnut bur; and my eyes, like the sherry in the glass, that the guest leaves. Would this do just as well?

"It often alarms father. He says death might occur, and he has moulds of all the rest, but has no mould of me; but I noticed the quick wore off those things, in a few days, and forestall the dishonor."

The tyranny of the visible makes us blind. The brilliance of the word pierces the night of the world.

THE DISTANCE FROM LAUGHTER TO MURDER is never far. In December 1876 Higginson attended a soirée at the Waring residence to celebrate their wedding anniversary yet again. For the event, the Woolseys, a couple fond of pranks, wrote texts adapted to each guest. Higginson had been telling them for some time now about his "partially cracked poetess," and now they handed to him a fake letter from Emily. There was whole-hearted laughter all around. A few months later Higginson's wife was gravely ill, and the partially cracked poetess offered her help, sending her a jasmine flower. "I send you a flower from my garden—Though it dies in reaching you, you will know it lived, when it left my hand." Emily did not realize that she was giving her jasmine to a woman who had publicly deplored the fact that her husband had attracted a madwoman.

Those who are most sensitive will always lose. They are God's chosen ones; he wipes their faces splattered silver with spit.

EMILY'S DESK DRAWERS WERE OPENED AFTER her death. A great light came from them, and Austin wanted to show it to the world—not without first adding a few shadows, necessary to preserve the family's modesty. As a good Dickinson, eager to have the entire world within reach, Austin had given Mabel Todd and her husband, David, a plot in the field adjoining the Evergreens on which to build their house. He spent his nights there with his mistress. When David returned at dawn, at the end of his night shift at the observatory, he hummed a tune to give Austin time to leave. It would take little Millicent Todd years to understand the sinister reason behind the song that woke her every morning.

It was in this house with its thirteen rooms that Emily's poems first entered the world. Vinnie crossed the meadow with a firm step several days in a row, carrying the big basket meant for firewood now filled willy-nilly with Emily's texts, which she spilled onto the floor in front of the fireplace in the Todds' parlor. On her knees, Mabel began the difficult task of sorting and classifying everything. The poems dedicated to Susan, on the other hand, did not leave Emily's house; like dangerous criminals, or the severely wounded, they could not be transported. Mabel stayed there to copy them out.

"The Air is soft as Italy, but when it touches me, I spurn it, because it is not you." These words, and others that Emily had written to Judge Lord, escaped Austin's scissors. Now that the man to whom they were destined was no more than bones and dry dust in a tomb, Emily's words wandered in search of a soul to beguile;

they leapt up before the reader's eyes, who discovered a love that speaks of "Bankruptcy" and "Crime" and "Realms of Ermine."

Otis Phillips Lord had sometimes attended the festivities that illuminated the Dickinsons' vast garden. He was eighteen years older than Emily. Married, childless, with his close friend Edward he shared a starched virtue. He was a supreme court judge for the state of Massachusetts, a pugnacious, ironic orator, a master at sparring with his adversaries. His principles were made of steel, his sentences of fire, and he did not hesitate to imprison any witness who refused to kiss the Bible upon taking the oath. Emily's love for this incorruptible horseman of the Apocalypse burst open upon Edward's death. Because the judge had been very close to her father at that time, to Emily this proximity conferred on him a halo bright with the clarity of the beyond, as if he had been splashed with light from the Everlasting. Henceforth he would inspire in her "a veneration … a primitive kind of awe." Sensing that a marvelous disaster was about to happen, the guardian of the tablets of stone erected a few fragile breakwaters. "Judge Lord was with us a few days since—and told me the Joy we most revere—we profane in taking. I wish that was wrong."

In 1877 the death of the judge's wife—added to Edward's passing and her mother's paralysis—would cause the dams of Puritanism to burst, and Emily, utterly astonished, would come to realize, rather late in life, that she had a soul incarnate. The figures of her father and of the man she loved were superimposed, and this gave rise to a feverish peace. "The exultation floods me. I cannot find my channel—the Creek turns Sea—at thought of thee." Fascinated by introspection, gifted with a sunny sense of humor, the judge revered Shakespeare above all others, for his intuitive grasp of fugitive spirits. Emily's spirit trembled in his

74

hands. She no longer identified herself, as she had for so long, with Julia Mills in *David Copperfield*, "interested in others' loves, herself withdrawn." She now had the febrile grace of a young woman in love and the same religious fervor for infinitesimal relics of feeling. "I will not wash my arm—the one you gave the scarf to—it is brown as an Almond—'twill take your touch away." Susan was furious to see Emily so joyful when she herself was not the cause. "You will not allow your husband to go there, I hope!" she said to Mabel. "They have not, either of them, any idea of morality. I went in there one day, and in the drawing room I found Emily reclining in the arms of a man." The cheeks of the lady in white were flushed; life fills with rainbows when we leave aside the habits with which we endeavor to subdue it.

"I feel like wasting my Cheek on your Hand tonight." Emily's every word drums upon the page, like the heart of a rabbit when one opens the cage to kill him, wrenching him from his torpor among the dried grasses. Words of love are words of distress—the cry of a little girl who in the night thought she saw a light on the craggy face of a widowed judge and man of letters.

EMILY HURRIED TO TOM KELLY, the Dickinsons' handyman, a bearded giant, and buried her face in his blue velvet jacket, letting her heart "break there—that was the warmest place." On that day in May 1882, she had just learned that Judge Lord was gravely ill. In November of that same year she would make a joking allusion to a marriage. As she had put on a bit of weight, the judge teased her by calling her Jumbo. "Emily 'Jumbo'!" she cried. "Sweetest name, but I know a sweeter—Emily Jumbo Lord. Have I your approval?" The judge replied favorably, but his family clenched their teeth and no one would ever speak of it again, on one side or the other. The wedding would never take place.

Little Millicent said she always felt "demeaned" when she looked at her mother, Mabel Todd's, hands: on her left hand she used to wear a diamond wedding band along with other precious rings. Now, since the beginning of her affair with Austin, all the rings, with the exception of the wedding band, had been moved to the right hand, as if to celebrate a clandestine wedding—or to remove the wedding ring from what surrounded it, "cleaning" it by making it supernaturally virginal and capable of symbolizing a forbidden union. For a long time Martha Dickinson, Susan and Austin's daughter, would keep a ring that had belonged to her aunt Emily; around the inside was etched Judge Lord's shortened middle name, "Phillip." Whether on the finger of an adulterous woman or that of a recluse, those rings stood for a union society disapproved of and that the heavens could not have broken.

WHEN TYPHOID FEVER STRUCK SUSAN AND AUSTIN'S lastborn child on October 5, 1883, their house collapsed into the invisible province where its true foundations lay. Austin wandered half-mad through the rubble of his soul, disgusted by his erstwhile rage to live. He once had the powerful jaw of a wild beast: the risk was great if one tried to wrench one's hunk of meat from him. Now the marble blow of death had obliged him to drop his imaginary prey.

Emily and the dying child had more than a usual complicity. Gilbert was Emily's double. They had the same crucifying sensibility. When one of his friends moved away from Amherst, the boy could not bear to see his portrait; to suffer less from his friend's absence, he asked that the picture be turned to face the wall. Life was an uninterrupted flow of wrenching loss, causing aunt and nephew to know the same trembling, the overwhelming grace of never getting used to anything.

Little Gilbert, in a photograph taken when he was alive, seems painfully intelligent. He has a girl's long blond hair. He is seated on an armchair that has been draped with a slipcover of the kind one finds in houses deserted by their owners. His hands are slightly tense. Our hands do not know how to hold onto anything on this earth. Our possessions are the dross of our future death. Only the soul should matter. Little Gilbert's would never be older than eight years of age.

"OPEN THE DOOR, OPEN THE DOOR, they're waiting for me!" raved the child, in a language that seemed to have been borrowed from one of his aunt's poems. He was more richly accompanied in his dying than Louis XIV, whose servants bellowed the king's name to stop the courtiers' cackling as he approached. An angel in ethereal livery announced the child's goodness to the invisible, opening the doors of heaven to him one by one until he reached the golden room. The body drained of its soul is nothing more than a rag doll. The useless, reassuring bustle of mourning began. Emily felt nauseous at the smell of disinfectant and returned to her home at three o'clock in the morning; she was sick, could not return to the funeral wake, and stayed in bed, her head engulfed by a burning migraine.

Two weeks after the funeral the *Amherst Record*, the local newspaper, painted the portrait of a little saint on a bicycle who went up to all those he met as he rode through the village and spoke to them with the utmost gravity. "The best in people he brought to the surface" the newspaper tells us; those he met were able to air out their Sunday soul, the one that almost never leaves the house.

All saints have some secret sin. This child loved to steal roses from his aunt's garden. One day Emily came upon his footprints in a border; from God she borrowed humor and from her father the demeanor of a man of law. She went discreetly to find the child's boots, polished them, put them upon a silver platter, filled them with fresh flowers, and had them carried over to the rose thief in the house next door, along with her calling card.

As he died Gilbert clung to Emily's soul—the way one clings to a tablecloth to slow one's fall, pulling everything off the table. All Emily's joy fell to the floor.

"Each of us takes heaven into our body or removes it, for each of us possesses the talent for living." But talent is nothing more than courage. Henceforth everything would be wrenched from an encroaching silence. In speaking of her mother, Emily said that on dying she "slipped from our fingers like a flake gathered by the wind, and is now part of the drift called 'the infinite.'" This drift entered Emily's room in her lifetime; her handwriting became more and more airy, streaked with emptiness. Words were split ever farther apart by this whiteness, then the letters between the words. Judge Lord's death a few months after little Gilbert's perfected the void. By wrenching from her those she loved, God left in Emily's soul a poison that she neither wanted nor knew how to expel. Depression set in, a kidney ailment. The lady in white turned to face the darkest night, "sitting," said Susan, "in the light of her own fire." She removed heaven from her body.

EMILY'S LIFE WAS SPECTACULARLY INVISIBLE. All spectacles die in the boredom they had hoped to exorcise. The only one that will never make us weary is that of a heart so pure that a bee can fly through it like a bullet, and nothing of the outside world can enter.

The inseparable Norcross cousins would receive the last of the hundreds of letters that Emily wrote—two words falling from the dying soul, like snowdrops at the foot of a cherry tree: "Called back."

In the obituary Susan wrote for the local paper, emphasis was placed on Emily's gifts for gardening—her writing talent scarcely mentioned. An Amherst resident, after reading the death notice that confirmed to him that he was well and truly alive, recalled for a few seconds the woman who had dazzled the sky with her camellias and jasmines, then he moved on to something else, unaware as he turned the page of the newspaper that he had just laid to rest the saint of the everyday.

CPSIA information can be obtained at www.ICGtesting.com
Printed in the USA
LVOW08s1152031014

407123LV00003B/5/P